P9-BIS-625

An EARLY I CAN READ Book

Mother Rabbit's Son Tom

by Dick Gackenbach

Harper & Row, Publishers
New York, Hagerstown, San Francisco, London

For Jim Murphy

MOTHER RABBIT'S SON TOM
Copyright © 1977 by Dick Gackenbach

All rights reserved. No part of this book may be used or reproduced in any manner whatsoever without written permission except in the case of brief quotations embodied in critical articles and reviews. Printed in the United States of America. For information address Harper & Row, Publishers, Inc., 10 East 53rd Street, New York, N.Y. 10022. Published simultaneously in Canada by Fitzhenry & Whiteside Limited, Toronto.

Library of Congress Cataloging in Publication Data
Gackenbach, Dick.
    Mother Rabbit's son Tom.

    (An Early I can read book)
    SUMMARY: Tom keeps Mother and Father Rabbit busy by asking for hamburgers and pets.
    [1.   Parent and child—Fiction.   2.   Rabbits—Fiction]
I.   Title.
PZ7.G117Mo   [E]   76-18399
ISBN 0-06-021947-5
ISBN 0-06-021948-3 lib. bdg.

Hamburgers,
Hamburgers

In sweet spring,

Mother Rabbit told Tom,

"Now is the time

to eat the tender dandelions."

"I want a hamburger," said Tom.

"With onions and ketchup

and pickles

on a poppy-seed roll."

Mother Rabbit shook her head.

"Oh dear," she said.

"I wish I had a nickel

for every pickle you eat."

In bright summer,

clover filled the fields.

"Eat some, Tom," Mother Rabbit said.

"The sun has made it

fresh and crisp."

But Tom wanted a hamburger
with onions and ketchup and pickles
on a poppy-seed roll.

"If you eat one more hamburger,"
Mother Rabbit said,
"your tail
will turn into an onion."

7

Autumn came
and frost filled the air.
Mother Rabbit told Tom,
"Have some good white corn.
It is ripe now."

"No corn!" said Tom.

"I want a hamburger

with onions and ketchup

and pickles

on a poppy-seed roll."

Mother Rabbit

looked into Tom's eyes.

"I thought so," she said.

"Your head is full of ketchup."

Mother Rabbit was worried.

She spoke to Tom's father.

"Someday

our son will turn into

one great big hamburger."

"Yes," said Father Rabbit.

"And his head

will look like

a poppy-seed roll."

11

In icy winter,

down under the snow,

Mother Rabbit

made a nut-and-berry stew.

"A fine dish for supper,"

she said.

"No thank you," said Tom.

"I know," sighed his mother.

"You want a hamburger!"

"Yes," said Tom.

"With onions and ketchup

and pickles

on a poppy-seed roll."

13

Early one morning

Mother Rabbit went to wake Tom.

There was a big lump

in his bed.

"What is this?"

she asked.

She peeked under the covers.

"Father!" she called.

"Come as fast as you can."

Father Rabbit

hurried to Tom's bed.

"Look!" said Mother Rabbit.

"Our Tom

has finally turned into

a hamburger!"

"Well," said Father Rabbit.

"What do you think of that?"

"I still love him, though,"

said Mother Rabbit.

"Oh, I do too," said Father Rabbit,

"even if his head

does look like

a poppy-seed roll."

They both laughed.

And Tom laughed most of all.

Tom's Pet

"Mother,

may I keep a dog?"

asked Tom.

"No!"

said his mother.

20

"I am sorry, Dog,"

said Tom,

"you cannot stay here."

"Mother,"

asked Tom,

"may I keep a cat?"

"You may not,"

said his mother.

"Sorry, Cat,"

said Tom.

"She said no."

"May I keep a chicken, Mother?"
asked Tom.

"No! No! No!" said his mother.

24

"I cannot have a chicken,"

said Tom.

"Humph!" said Chicken.

25

"How about a frog?"

asked Tom.

"Please get that thing

out of the house,"

said his mother.

"So long,"

said Tom.

"I do not think

she likes frogs."

"May I keep a dinosaur, Mother?"

asked Tom.

"There are no dinosaurs,"

said his mother.

"If there *were* dinosaurs,

could I keep one?" he asked.

"Yes," laughed his mother,

"you could keep one."

29